OVERGROUND RAILROAD

LESA CLINE-RANSOME   JAMES RANSOME

HOLIDAY HOUSE · NEW YORK

HOLIDAY HOUSE is registered in the U.S. Patent and Trademark Office.
Printed and bound in September 2019 at Worzalla Publishers, Stevens Point, WI, USA.
This book was illustrated with paper, graphite, paste pencils, and watercolors.
www.holidayhouse.com
First Edition
1 3 5 7 9 10 8 6 4 2

Library of Congress Cataloging-in-Publication Data
Names: Cline-Ransome, Lesa, author. | Ransome, James, illustrator.
Title: Overground railroad / by Lesa Cline-Ransome ; illustrated by James Ransome.
Description: First edition. | New York : Holiday House, [2020] | Summary: "A
girl named Ruth Ellen tells the story of her family's train journey from
North Carolina to New York City as part of the Great Migration"—Provided by publisher.
Identifiers: LCCN 2019021547 | ISBN 9780823438730 (hardback)
Subjects: | CYAC: African Americans—Migrations—Fiction. | African
Americans—History—Fiction. | Railroad travel—Fiction. | BISAC: JUVENILE
FICTION / People & Places / United States / African American. | JUVENILE
FICTION / Historical / United States / 20th Century. | JUVENILE FICTION /Stories in Verse.
Classification: LCC PZ7.C622812 Ov 2020 | DDC [E]—dc23
LC record available at https://lccn.loc.gov/2019021547
ISBN: 978-0-8234-3873-0

To Isabel Wilkerson,
your words provide endless
inspiration . . .
—L.C.R.

In memory of John Christopher Pruitt
(July 1952–June 2019)
—J.E.R.

Some walked.
Some drove.
But we took the train north.
Me and Mama and Daddy got to the station
crack of dawn early
before anyone
could see us leave.
Daddy holding tight
to me with one hand
three tickets to New York in the other.

The porter helped us on board
then handed us our bags
and our shoebox
filled with food
and tied with string
onto the first train out of North Carolina
just as the conductor yelled,

"All Aboard
the New York Bound Silver Meteor!"

Daddy led me to the last seats
in the colored car
and let me sit
next to the window
to watch
as the train whistled
and chugged
leaving puffs of smoke
behind.

We left in secret
before Daddy's boss knew,
before our lease was up.
We said our goodbyes
to Uncle Buck and Granddaddy
and Grandma
her wet cheek
pressed against mine.
"Ruth Ellen, you mind your mama and daddy,"
she said.

"No more picking,"
Daddy said mad.

"No more working someone else's land,"
Mama said proud.
"We're gonna make our own way up North,"
they both said.

Out the window
I watched
Blue Ridge Mountains
and fields with folks
already hunched and picking
row after row
of cotton, tobacco, and peanuts
every day
except the Lord's day
just like my granddaddy
but not anymore for my daddy.

At the next stop
more people
and boxes
and satchels
squeezed into
the colored car
so many
they stood
on tired feet
or sat
on hard floors
where they were.

Daddy pulled out cards
to pass the time.
I won at rummy
Daddy at war.
In my bag
is the book
Teacher pressed in my hands
on my last day of school
before we left.

"Next Stop Norfolk, Virginia!"

In our straight-back seats
when we finish with cards
Mama fusses in her purse
Daddy stares ahead
I take out the book
Teacher gave me.
The cover's worn,
pages too.
"Read to me, Ruthie," Mama says
and I do.
First the title,
"Narrative of the Life of
Frederick Douglass."

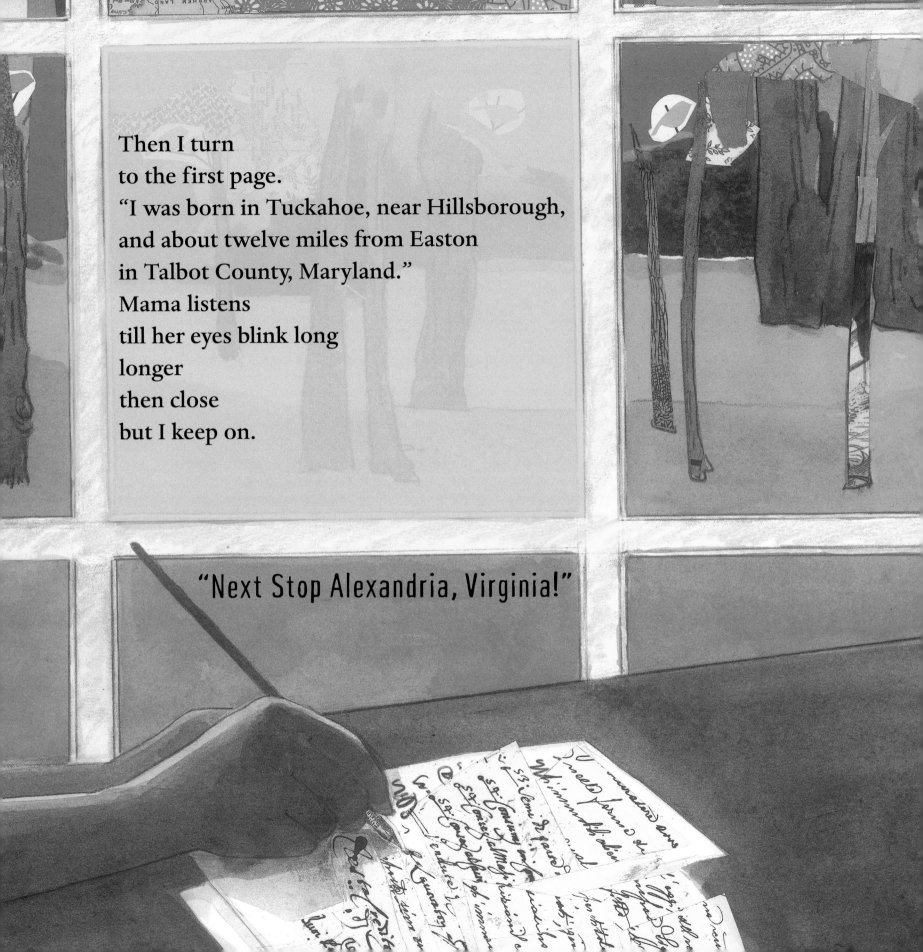

Then I turn
to the first page.
"I was born in Tuckahoe, near Hillsborough,
and about twelve miles from Easton
in Talbot County, Maryland."
Mama listens
till her eyes blink long
longer
then close
but I keep on.

"Next Stop Alexandria, Virginia!"

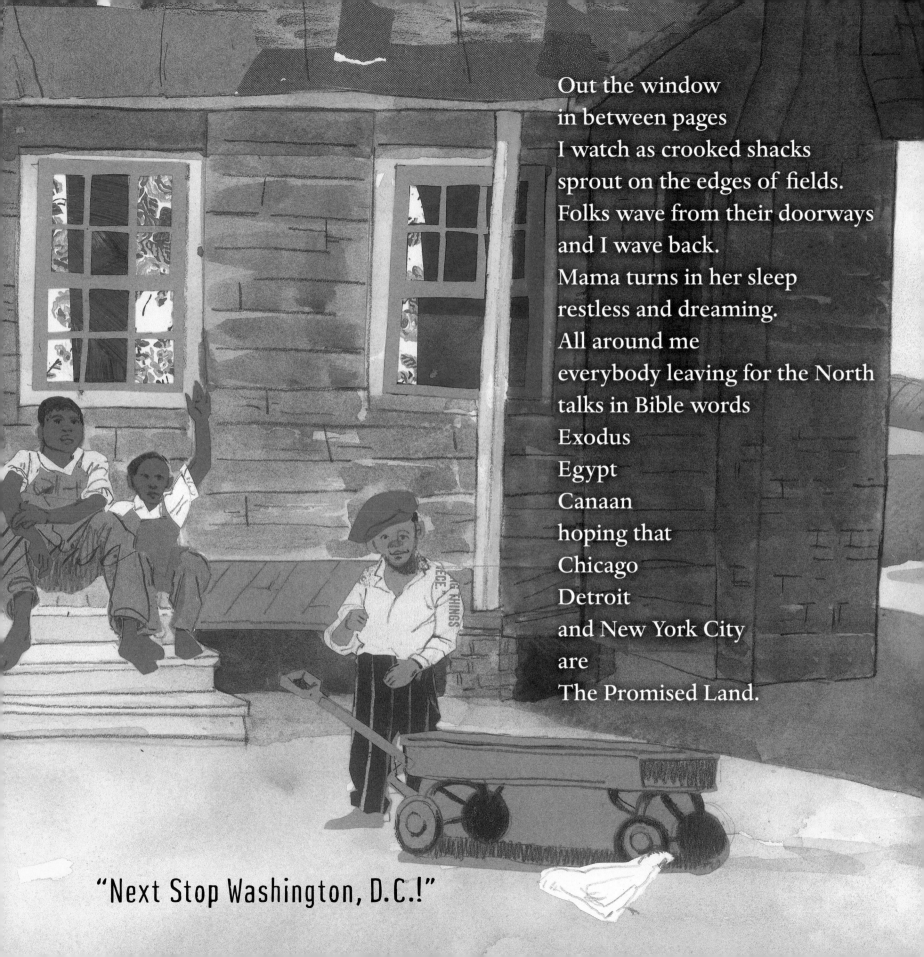

Out the window
in between pages
I watch as crooked shacks
sprout on the edges of fields.
Folks wave from their doorways
and I wave back.
Mama turns in her sleep
restless and dreaming.
All around me
everybody leaving for the North
talks in Bible words
Exodus
Egypt
Canaan
hoping that
Chicago
Detroit
and New York City
are
The Promised Land.

"Next Stop Washington, D.C.!"

The porters come and move signs
waking Daddy
telling everyone in the colored section
to sit where they want.
We don't have to stay
in front behind the engine
breathing in smoke
'cause we're past the line
that divides black from white
south from north
wrong from right.
I wait to move but we wait more.
Finally
Daddy takes my hand and Mama stands
and we walk down the aisle
out the colored car
and through the curtain.

"Next Stop Baltimore, Maryland!"

On the other side of the curtain
is the dining car
with tablecloths
and clinking glasses
and white faces
and good food smells
that make my stomach growl
and make me wish
we hadn't eaten
Grandma's fried chicken
and hard boiled eggs
and lemon pound cake
so soon.

"Next Stop Newark, Delaware!"

We walk past
row after row
of white folks
who stare or turn away
with eyes that say
keep moving
when they see us

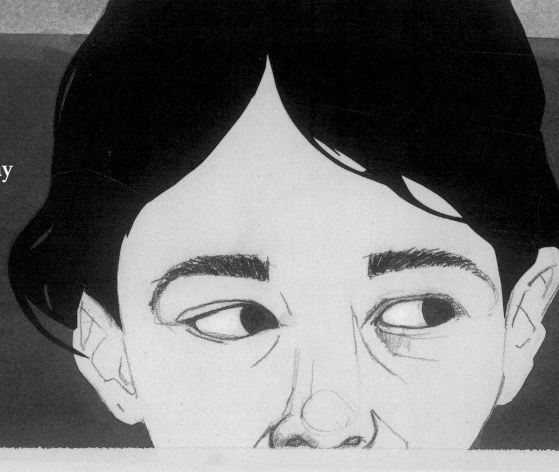

some put hands in empty seats
not here
and we keep walking
until we find
smiles
from new neighbors.

Out the window
people turn and point
and I see water
a whole river
running long beside us.
"It's the Delaware River,"
a mother says to her boy.
The book Teacher gave me
has pages filled
with the story of a boy
leaving behind what he knew
and heading to what he don't
just like me
only he didn't have a ticket
bought by his daddy
and food packed by his grandma

so he was cold and hungry
but he kept on running
at night
with only
the North Star to guide him
along the Chesapeake
and the Delaware River
in secret
getting help along the way
till he made his way walking
to freedom
North.

I watch the tracks
in front of me
and behind me
just as far
as the eye can see.
Mama and Daddy say
jobs
education
freedom
are waiting in New York for us.
And like the boy in the book
we all running from
and running to
at the same time.

"Last Stop New York City, Penn Station!"

We step off the train
and I stretch my neck to see
bright lights
tall buildings
shimmering against a sky
bright as a hundred North Stars.
Daddy grabs our bags
I squeeze Mama's hand
the other
holds tight
to my book.

AUTHOR'S NOTE

After writing about the lives of Frederick Douglass and Harriet Tubman, I was very familiar with the intricate and elaborate network called the Underground Railroad. But I'd certainly never heard of the Overground Railroad, a term I discovered after reading Isabel Wilkerson's *The Warmth of Other Suns*. The Overground Railroad refers to the railway system that carried millions of blacks who left the South during the Great Migration. At times, this system was as much a covert operation as the Underground Railroad, as the owners of farms who operated tenant farms, also called sharecropping, used threats of violence and other tactics to prevent workers from leaving. The sharecropping system kept many of its black tenants perpetually in debt

to their landlords and made it "illegal" to leave without permission or before repaying the debts incurred for planting and other supplies. As a result, many blacks departed on trains north under the cover of night or secretly boarded trains miles from home in neighboring towns for the chance at better employment, education, and a life in the North free from oppression.

Overground Railroad is inspired by just one of the many stories of people who were running from and running to at the same time . . .

Lesa Cline-Ransome